Escape from Slavery

Escape from Slavery

The Boyhood of Frederick Douglass
in His Own Words

Edited and illustrated by
MICHAEL McCURDY

Foreword by
Coretta Scott King

ALFRED A. KNOPF
New York

THIS IS A BORZOI BOOK PUBLISHED BY ALFRED A. KNOPF, INC.

Book design by Mina Greenstein
Manufactured in the United States of America
10 11 12 13 14 15 16 17 18 19

Library of Congress Cataloging-in-Publication Data
Douglass, Frederick, 1817?–1895.
Escape from slavery: the boyhood of Frederick Douglass in his own words /
edited and illustrated by Michael McCurdy.
p. cm.
Rev. ed. of: The narrative of the life of Frederick Douglass,
an American slave. 1845.
Summary: A shortened autobiography presenting the early life of the slave who
became an abolitionist, journalist, and statesman.
ISBN 0-679-84652-2 (trade)   ISBN 0-679-84651-4 (pbk)
1. Douglass, Frederick, 1817?–1895—Childhood and youth—Juvenile literature.
2. Slaves—United States—Biography—Juvenile literature.   3. Afro-Americans—
Biography—Juvenile literature.   4. Abolitionists—United States—Biography—
Juvenile literature.
[1. Douglass, Frederick, 1817?–1895.   2. Slaves.   3. Afro-Americans—Biography.
4. Abolitionists.]   I. McCurdy, Michael.   II. Douglass, Frederick, 1817?–1895.
Narrative of the life of Frederick Douglass, an American slave.   III. Title.
E449.D749   1994   973.8'092—dc20   [B]   93-19239

To MICHELE RUBIN, who had the idea,
to DEBORAH McCURDY, who helped develop it,
and to ANNE SCHWARTZ, who made it possible

Foreword

FREDERICK DOUGLASS was never President of the United States, or a Congressman. He never even attended school. But as an eloquent spokesman and a superb strategist in the struggle against slavery, he had a tremendous influence on the growth of American democracy.

In Douglass's autobiography of his early years, *Narrative of the Life of Frederick Douglass, An American Slave, Written by Himself,* he reveals the proud, courageous spirit that made him one of the greatest freedom fighters in history. Born into slavery, separated from his family, and forced to suffer frequent beatings and humiliation from slave masters, Douglass might easily have become just another among the millions of slaves whose condition denied a chance for a decent life. But like my husband, Martin Luther King, Jr., who was inspired and deeply moved by these writings, young Frederick had a dream that one day he and all black people would live in freedom.

This gripping story of how he finally achieved his freedom

provides one of the best firsthand descriptions of slavery ever written. Douglass was one of the finest writers and speakers of his time, and there is much we can still learn from the way he used language as a tool for liberation.

In *Escape from Slavery: The Boyhood of Frederick Douglass in His Own Words,* Michael McCurdy, determined to bring Douglass's writing to a new generation of readers, has done a wonderful job of editing and illustrating the autobiography. As you read and enjoy this important book, your understanding of slavery and your appreciation of this great American will be immeasurably enriched.

—*Coretta Scott King*
1994

Introduction

THE MAN THE WORLD CAME TO KNOW as Frederick Douglass was born into slavery around 1817 (the exact date is in question) and given the name Frederick Augustus Washington Bailey. His mother was a slave, and his father was probably his mother's white owner. From an early age Douglass had an intense desire to learn how to read, an awareness of what the evils of slavery did to both blacks and whites, and a constant vision of freedom that sustained him.

When Douglass was born, there were about 1.5 million slaves—men, women, and children—in the United States. Ten years before his birth, their importation from Africa and elsewhere had been outlawed. In practice, however, slave ships continued to dock at American ports until 1864.

Every year thousands of slaves managed to escape from their owners—an extremely dangerous undertaking. In 1793 the first fugitive slave law had made it illegal to help slaves run away, and fugitives were often found, arrested, and returned to the

South. It was not until eight months after President Abraham Lincoln's death in 1865 that slavery was formally abolished in the United States.

At the age of twenty Frederick Douglass escaped his bonds and eventually rose against all odds to become one of this country's first great African-American abolitionists—and also one of the first male advocates of a woman's right to vote.

On August 16, 1841, Douglass attended an antislavery meeting on Nantucket Island in Massachusetts. He rose to speak. Douglass had never addressed a predominantly white audience before, and he was nervous. His words came from the heart. He told of his bitter life in slavery and of the cruelty, beatings, and terrible living conditions of his brothers and sisters in the faraway South. His voice found strength to match his conviction, and the audience was deeply moved.

Douglass was urged by his listeners to put his talents to use in the Abolitionist cause, the growing antislavery movement. And that was the beginning of Douglass's life as a great speaker, writer, and founder of the Abolitionist newspaper *The North Star*. During the Civil War he supported the use of African Americans as soldiers in the Union Army, and he helped raise two Negro regiments. He knew that young black men—including his own two sons—would prove to be dedicated comrades-in-arms against a tyranny they knew all too well.

In 1870 Douglass supported President Ulysses S. Grant's plan to create a homeland for American blacks on the Caribbean island of Santo Domingo (now called the Dominican Republic). Douglass was appointed secretary of the Santo Domingo Commission. The plan did not succeed, however. In 1876 he was appointed marshal of the District of Columbia, the first appointment of a black man requiring Senate approval. In 1889 he became the second African American to serve as United States Ambassador to Haiti. Douglass died in 1895, after fifty-seven years of living as a free man and helping others to freedom.

WHAT FOLLOWS is my shortened version of the first of Douglass's three autobiographies, *Narrative of the Life of Frederick Douglass, An American Slave, Written by Himself.* Though Douglass had been taken seriously by many well-known white people of his day, there were those who couldn't believe that someone so eloquent and educated had ever been a slave. Written in part to address these skeptics, *Narrative* was published in Boston by the Anti-Slavery Office in June 1845 and sold for fifty cents a copy. The famous abolitionist William Lloyd Garrison wrote the preface, and Wendell Phillips, the Boston reformer who had urged Douglass to tell his story, wrote a letter for the first edition to help attract the attention of a white audience.

This edition is shorter than the original, to emphasize action and events for a younger audience. I have kept Douglass's own words, spelling, and distinctive punctuation (except for deleting the occasional comma he would use before a dash). Douglass's paragraphs and chapters have occasionally been broken up for the sake of clarity. Chapter notes have been added to provide background and to summarize the omitted sections. I hope this book will spark your interest in this great American so that you will want to read his complete *Narrative* at a later time.

WHEN I FIRST READ Douglass's *Narrative,* I was deeply moved by the searing injustice exposed on every page. I felt that his story had to be brought to younger readers, in both words and images. I wanted young people to know what had once happened to their African-American brothers and sisters; I wanted them to see the evils of intolerance and distrust that haunted Frederick Douglass more than a century ago and that still exist in our own time. But most of all I wanted to share Douglass's inspiring message: that a truly dedicated young person can—with the help of friends—break free from any bonds and help others to freedom.

—*Michael McCurdy*
1994

Escape from Slavery

ONE

FREDERICK DOUGLASS *was born in a small cabin near Hills-borough (now spelled Hillsboro), in Talbot County, Maryland, probably in 1817. He spent his early childhood on one of the thirteen farms that made up Edward Lloyd's immense wheat-producing plantation. Lloyd's chief manager, Aaron Anthony, was Frederick's first owner.*

The cabin where Frederick lived was built of rough slabs of bark, with a floor made from the clay of nearby Tuckahoe Creek. As a small boy, he had no privacy in the cramped cabin that he shared with several cousins, two younger sisters, his grandparents Betsey and Isaac Bailey, and his grandmother's little son. To enable her daughters to work on the plantation, Betsey was expected to care for their children. She was a slave, but Isaac was a freeman. The family may originally have been brought from the West Indies to be sold to Maryland tobacco farmers.

Frederick's early years were relatively carefree. He explored the woods and creek around the cabin and enjoyed a loving home life. All this was to change abruptly when at the age of six he was sent to live in his owner's house. He accompanied his grandmother on the long walk, unaware of what was about to happen. Soon after their arrival, she left quietly, without Frederick knowing, until one of the children at his new home cried, ''Fed, Fed! Grandmammy gone, Grandmammy gone!''

I have no accurate knowledge of my age. By far the larger part of the slaves know as little of their ages as horses know of theirs, and it is the wish of most masters within my knowledge to keep their slaves thus ignorant. I do not remember to have ever met a slave who could tell of his birthday.

My mother was named Harriet Bailey. My father was a white man. The opinion was also whispered that my master was my father; but of the correctness of this opinion, I know nothing; the means of knowing was withheld from me. My mother and I were separated when I was but an infant.

I never saw my mother, to know her as such, more than four or five times in my life; and each of these times was very short in duration, and at night. She was hired by a Mr. Stewart, who lived about twelve miles from my home. She made her journeys to see me in the night, travelling the whole distance on foot, after the performance of her day's work. She was a field hand, and a whipping is the penalty of not being in the field at sunrise, unless a slave has special permission from his or her master to the contrary.

She was with me in the night. She would lie down with me, and get me to sleep, but long before I waked she was gone.

Very little communication ever took place between us. Death

soon ended what little we could have while she lived, and with it her hardships and suffering. She died when I was about seven years old, on one of my master's farms, near Lee's Mill. I was not allowed to be present during her illness, at her death, or burial. She was gone long before I knew any thing about it. Never having enjoyed, to any considerable extent, her soothing presence, her tender and watchful care, I received the tidings of her death with much the same emotions I should have probably felt at the death of a stranger.

MEN AND WOMEN SLAVES RECEIVED, as their monthly allowance of food, eight pounds of pork, or its equivalent in fish, and one bushel of corn meal. Their yearly clothing consisted of two coarse linen shirts, one pair of linen trousers, like the shirts, one jacket, one pair of trousers for winter, made of coarse negro cloth, one pair of stockings, and one pair of shoes; the whole of which could not have cost more than seven dollars.

The children unable to work in the field had neither shoes, stockings, jackets, nor trousers, given to them; their clothing consisted of two coarse linen shirts per year. When these failed them, they went naked. Children from seven to ten years old, of both sexes, almost naked, might be seen at all seasons of the year.

There were no beds given the slaves, unless one coarse blanket be considered such, and none but the men and women had these. They find less difficulty from the want of beds, than from the want of time to sleep; for when their day's work in the field is done, the most of them have their washing, mending, and cooking to do, and having few or none of the ordinary facilities for doing either of these, very many of their sleeping hours are consumed in preparing for the field the coming day;

and when this is done, old and young, male and female, married and single, drop down side by side, on one common bed—the cold, damp floor—each covering himself or herself with their miserable blankets; and here they sleep till they are summoned to the field by the driver's horn.

At the sound of this, all must rise, and be off to the field. There must be no halting; every one must be at his or her post; and woe betides them who hear not this morning summons to the field; for if they are not awakened by the sense of hearing, they are by the sense of feeling; no age nor sex finds any favor. Mr. Severe, the overseer, used to stand by the door of the quarter, armed with a large hickory stick and heavy cowskin, ready to whip any one who was so unfortunate as not to hear, or, from any other cause, was prevented from being ready to start for the field at the sound of the horn.

Few privileges were esteemed higher, by the slaves of the out-farms, than that of being selected to do errands at the Great House Farm. While on their way, they would make the dense old woods, for miles around, reverberate with their wild songs. I did not, when a slave, understand the deep meaning of those rude* and apparently incoherent songs. They told a tale of woe which was then altogether beyond my feeble comprehension; they were tones loud, long, and deep; they breathed the prayer and complaint of souls boiling over with the bitterest anguish. Every tone was a testimony against slavery, and a prayer to God for deliverance from chains.

I have often been utterly astonished, since I came to the north, to find persons who could speak of the singing, among slaves, as evidence of their contentment and happiness. It is

*By "rude" Douglass meant unpolished.

impossible to conceive of a greater mistake. Slaves sing most when they are most unhappy. The songs of the slave represent the sorrows of his heart; and he is relieved by them, only as an aching heart is relieved by its tears. At least, such is my experience. I have often sung to drown my sorrow, but seldom to express my happiness. Crying for joy, and singing for joy, were alike uncommon to me while in the jaws of slavery. The singing of a man cast away upon a desolate island might be as appropriately considered as evidence of contentment and happiness, as the singing of a slave; the songs of the one and of the other are prompted by the same emotion.

I WAS NOT OLD ENOUGH to work in the field, and there being little else than field work to do, I had a great deal of leisure time. The most I had to do was to drive up the cows at evening, keep the fowls out of the garden, keep the front yard clean, and run of errands for my old master's daughter, Mrs. Lucretia Auld. The most of my leisure time I spent in helping Master Daniel Lloyd in finding his birds, after he had shot them. My connection with Master Daniel was of some advantage to me. He became quite attached to me, and was a sort of protector of me. He would not allow the older boys to impose upon me, and would divide his cakes with me.

Our food was coarse corn meal boiled. This was called *mush*. It was put into a large wooden tray or trough, and set down upon the ground. The children were then called, like so many pigs, and like so many pigs they would come and devour the mush; some with oyster-shells, others with pieces of shingle, some with naked hands, and none with spoons. He that ate fastest got most; he that was strongest secured the best place; and few left the trough satisfied.

I suffered much from hunger, but much more from cold. In hottest summer and coldest winter, I was kept almost naked—no shoes, no stockings, no jacket, no trousers, nothing on but a coarse tow linen shirt, reaching only to my knees. I had no bed. I must have perished with cold, but that, the coldest nights, I used to steal a bag which was used for carrying corn to the mill. I would crawl into this bag, and there sleep on the cold, damp, clay floor, with my head in and feet out. My feet have been so cracked with the frost, that the pen with which I am writing might be laid in the gashes.

T W O

FREDERICK IS ABOUT eight years old when he is told that he will be sent to live in Baltimore with Hugh Auld, the brother of his owner's son-in-law. Frederick is given his first trousers and tuck-in shirt. Having been told that he will be laughed at in Baltimore if he is dirty, Frederick spends hours in the creek scrubbing the plantation dirt from his skin. Finally he is put on a boat with a flock of sheep that are destined to be slaughtered in Baltimore, and as he sails out of the Miles River toward the city, he takes what he hopes will be one last look at the plantation.

I found no severe trial in my departure. My home was charmless; it was not home to me; on parting from it, I could not feel that I was leaving any thing which I could have enjoyed by staying. My mother was dead, my grandmother lived far off, so that I seldom saw her. I had two sisters and one

brother, that lived in the same house with me; but the early separation of us from our mother had well nigh blotted the fact of our relationship from our memories. I looked for home elsewhere, and was confident of finding none which I should relish less than the one which I was leaving. If, however, I found in my new home hardship, hunger, whipping, and nakedness, I had the consolation that I should not have escaped any one of them by staying.

I may be deemed superstitious, and even egotistical, in regarding this event as a special interposition of divine Providence in my favor. But I should be false to the earliest sentiments of my soul, if I suppressed the opinion. I prefer to be true to myself, even at the hazard of incurring the ridicule of others, rather than to be false, and incur my own abhorrence. From my earliest recollection, I date the entertainment of a deep conviction that slavery would not always be able to hold me within its foul embrace; and in the darkest hours of my career in slavery, this living word of faith and spirit of hope departed not from me, but remained like ministering angels to cheer me through the gloom. This good spirit was from God, and to him I offer thanksgiving and praise.

WE ARRIVED AT BALTIMORE early on Sunday morning, landing at Smith's Wharf. I was conducted to my new home in Alliciana Street. Mr. and Mrs. Auld were both at home, and met me at the door with their little son Thomas, to take care of whom I had been given. And here I saw what I had never seen before; it was a white face beaming with the most kindly emotions; it was the face of my new mistress, Sophia Auld. It was a new and strange sight to me, brightening up my pathway with the light of happiness. Little Thomas was told, there was his Freddy—and I was told to take care of little Thomas; and thus I entered upon the duties of my new home with the most cheering prospect ahead.

My new mistress proved to be all she appeared when I first met her at the door—a woman of the kindest heart and finest feelings. She had never had a slave under her control previously to myself, and prior to her marriage she had been dependent upon her own industry for a living.

Very soon after I went to live with Mr. and Mrs. Auld, she very kindly commenced to teach me the A, B, C. After I had learned this, she assisted me in learning to spell words of three or four letters. Just at this point of my progress, Mr. Auld found out what was going on, and at once forbade Mrs. Auld to instruct me further, telling her, among other things, that it was unlawful, as well as unsafe, to teach a slave to read. To use his own words, he said, "If you give a nigger an inch, he will take an ell.* A nigger should know nothing but to obey his master—to do as he is told to do. Learning would *spoil* the best nigger in the world. Now," said he, "if you teach that nigger [speaking of myself] how to read, there would be no keeping him. It would forever unfit him to be a slave. He would at once become unmanageable, and of no value to his master."

These words sank deep into my heart, stirred up sentiments within that lay slumbering, and called into existence an entirely new train of thought. I now understood what had been to me a most perplexing difficulty—to wit, the white man's power to enslave the black man. From that moment, I understood the pathway from slavery to freedom. It was just what I wanted, and I got it at a time when I the least expected it. Whilst I was

*A measurement that is the equivalent of an arm's length.

saddened by the thought of losing the aid of my kind mistress, I was gladdened by the invaluable instruction which, by the merest accident, I had gained from my master. Though conscious of the difficulty of learning without a teacher, I set out with high hope, and a fixed purpose, at whatever cost of trouble, to learn how to read.

My mistress was, as I have said, a kind and tender-hearted woman. There was no sorrow or suffering for which she had not a tear. She had bread for the hungry, clothes for the naked, and comfort for every mourner that came within her reach. Slavery soon proved its ability to divest her of these heavenly qualities. Under its influence, the tender heart became stone, and the lamblike disposition gave way to one of tiger-like fierceness. The first step in her downward course was in her ceasing to instruct me. She now commenced to practise her husband's precepts. She finally became even more violent in her opposition than her husband. Nothing seemed to make her more angry than to see me with a newspaper. She seemed to think that here lay the danger. I have had her rush at me with a face made up of fury, and snatch from me a newspaper, in a manner that fully revealed her apprehension. She was an apt woman; and a little experience soon demonstrated, to her satisfaction, that education and slavery were incompatible with each other.

From this time I was most narrowly watched. If I was in a separate room any considerable length of time, I was sure to be suspected of having a book, and was at once called to give an account of myself. All this, however, was too late. The first step had been taken. Mistress, in teaching me the alphabet, had given me the *inch*, and no precaution could prevent me from taking the *ell*.

The plan which I adopted, and the one by which I was most successful, was that of making friends of all the little white boys whom I met in the street. As many of these as I could, I converted into teachers. With their kindly aid, obtained at different times and in different places, I finally succeeded in learning to read.

The more I read, the more I was led to abhor and detest my enslavers. I could regard them in no other light than a band of successful robbers, who had left their homes, and gone to Africa, and stolen us from our homes, and in a strange land reduced us to slavery. I loathed them as being the meanest as well as the most wicked of men. It opened my eyes to the horrible pit, but to no ladder upon which to get out. In moments of agony, I envied my fellow-slaves for their stupidity. I have often wished myself a beast. I preferred the condition of the meanest reptile to my own. Any thing, no matter what, to get rid of thinking! It was this everlasting thinking of my condition that tormented me. There was no getting rid of it. It was pressed upon me by every object within sight or hearing, animate or inanimate. The silver trump of freedom had roused my soul to eternal wakefulness. Freedom now appeared, to disappear no more forever. It was heard in every sound, and seen in every thing. It was ever present to torment me with a sense of my wretched condition. I saw nothing without seeing it, I heard nothing without hearing it, and felt nothing without feeling it. It looked from every star, it smiled in every calm, breathed in every wind, and moved in every storm.

T H R E E

Some time after Frederick's arrival in Baltimore, his old owner Aaron Anthony dies. As a result, the boy is sent for, to be included in the estate's valuation. Frederick is to become the property of Master Anthony's daughter Lucretia. However, Lucretia will die unexpectedly, and her husband Thomas Auld will become Frederick's new owner. Master Thomas will arrange for Frederick to be returned to the household of his brother, Hugh Auld. But the young slave's life will soon be disrupted again, as he is destined to become a helpless pawn in a family quarrel.

We were all ranked together at the valuation. Men and women, old and young, married and single, were ranked with horses, sheep, and swine. There were horses and men, cattle and women, pigs and children, all holding the same rank in the scale of being, and were all subjected to the same narrow examination. Silvery-headed age and sprightly youth,

maids and matrons, had to undergo the same indelicate inspection. At this moment, I saw more clearly than ever the brutalizing effects of slavery upon both slave and slaveholder.

After the valuation, then came the division. I have no language to express the high excitement and deep anxiety which were felt among us poor slaves during this time. Our fate for life was now to be decided. We had no more voice in that decision than the brutes among whom we were ranked. A single word from the white men was enough—against all our wishes, prayers, and entreaties—to sunder forever the dearest friends, dearest kindred, and strongest ties known to human beings.

If any one thing in my experience, more than another, served to deepen my conviction of the infernal character of slavery, and to fill me with unutterable loathing of slaveholders, it was their base ingratitude to my poor old grandmother. She had served my old master faithfully from youth to old age. She had been the source of all his wealth; she had peopled his plantation with slaves; she had become a great-grandmother in his service. She had rocked him in infancy, attended him in childhood, served him through life, and at his death wiped from his icy brow the cold death-sweat, and closed his eyes forever. She was nevertheless left a slave—a slave for life—a slave in the hands of strangers; and in their hands she saw her children, her grandchildren, and her great-grandchildren, divided, like so many sheep, without being gratified with the small privilege of a single word, as to their or her own destiny.

IN ABOUT TWO YEARS after the death of Mrs. Lucretia, Master Thomas married his second wife. Her name was Rowena Hamilton. Not long after his marriage, a misunderstanding took place between himself and Master Hugh; and as a means of punishing his brother, he took me from him to live with himself at St. Michael's. Here I underwent another most painful separation. It was not so severe as the one I dreaded at the division of property; for, during this interval, a great change had taken place in Master Hugh and his once kind and affectionate wife. The influence of brandy upon him, and of slavery upon her, had effected a disastrous change in the characters of both. I thought I had little to lose by the change.

But it was not to them that I was attached. It was to those little Baltimore boys that I felt the strongest attachment. I had received many good lessons from them, and the thought of leaving them was painful indeed.

I left Baltimore, and went to live again with Master Thomas Auld, at St. Michael's, in March, 1832. I was made acquainted with his wife not less than with himself. They were well matched, being equally mean and cruel. Bad as all slaveholders are, we seldom meet one destitute of every element of character commanding respect. My master was one of this rare sort. I do not know of one single noble act ever performed by him. The leading trait in his character was meanness.

Captain Auld was not born a slaveholder. He came into possession of all his slaves by marriage; and of all men, adopted slaveholders are the worst. He was cruel, but cowardly. He commanded without firmness. In the enforcement of his rules, he was at times rigid, and at times lax. The luxury of having slaves of his own to wait upon him was something new and unprepared for. He found himself incapable of managing his slaves either by force, fear, or fraud. We seldom called him "master;" we generally called him "Captain Auld," and were hardly disposed to title him at all.

I have seen him tie up a lame young woman, and whip her

with a heavy cowskin upon her naked shoulders, causing the warm red blood to drip; and, in justification of the bloody deed, he would quote this passage of Scripture—"He that knoweth his master's will, and doeth it not, shall be beaten with many stripes."

Master would keep this lacerated young woman tied up in this horrid situation four or five hours at a time. I have known him to tie her up early in the morning, and whip her before breakfast; leave her, go to his store, return at dinner, and whip her again, cutting her in the places already made raw with his cruel lash.

My master and myself had quite a number of differences. He found me unsuitable. My city life, he said, had had a pernicious effect upon me. It had almost ruined me for every good purpose, and fitted me for every thing which was bad.

I had lived with him nine months, during which time he had given me a number of severe whippings, all to no good purpose. He resolved to put me out, as he said, to be broken; and, for this purpose, he let me for one year to a man named Edward Covey. Mr. Covey was a poor man, a farm-renter. He rented the place upon which he lived, as also the hands with which he tilled it. Mr. Covey had acquired a very high reputation for breaking young slaves, and this reputation was of immense value to him.

F O U R

FREDERICK IS NOW almost sixteen years old, large and strong for his age. For the first time in his life he is a field hand, working for Edward Covey. As a country boy in Baltimore and in the town of St. Michaels, Frederick had felt awkward and unsophisticated. Now, accustomed to city and town life, he finds that he is unsuited for hard labor. He has no knowledge of farm animals, and he is frightened by the large draft horses and teams of oxen.

I had been at my new home but one week before Mr. Covey gave me a very severe whipping, cutting my back, causing the blood to run, and raising ridges on my flesh as large as my little finger.

The details of this affair are as follows: Mr. Covey sent me, very early in the morning of one of our coldest days in the month of January, to the woods, to get a load of wood. He gave me a team of unbroken oxen. He told me which was the in-hand ox, and which the off-hand one. He then tied the end of a large rope around the horns of the in-hand ox, and gave me the other end of it, and told me, if the oxen started to run, that I must hold on upon the rope. I had never driven oxen before, and of course I was very awkward. I, however, succeeded in getting to the edge of the woods with little difficulty; but I had got a very few rods* into the woods, when the oxen took fright, and started full tilt, carrying the cart against trees, and over stumps, in the most frightful manner. I expected every moment that my brains would be dashed out against the trees. After running thus for a considerable distance, they finally upset the cart, dashing it with great force against a tree, and threw themselves into a dense thicket. How I escaped death, I do not know. There I was, entirely alone, in a thick wood, in a place new to me. My cart was upset and shattered, my oxen were entangled among the young trees, and there was none to help me. After a long spell of effort, I succeeded in getting my cart righted, my oxen disentangled, and again yoked to the cart.

I now proceeded with my team to the place where I had, the day before, been chopping wood, and loaded my cart pretty heavily, thinking in this way to tame my oxen. I then proceeded on my way home. I had now consumed one half of the day. I got out of the woods safely, and now felt out of danger. I stopped my oxen to open the woods gate; and just as I did so, before I could get hold of my ox-rope, the oxen again started, rushed through the gate, catching it between the wheel and the body of the cart, tearing it to pieces, and coming within a few inches of crushing me against the gate-post. Thus twice, in one

*A rod is a measure of length equal to sixteen and a half feet.

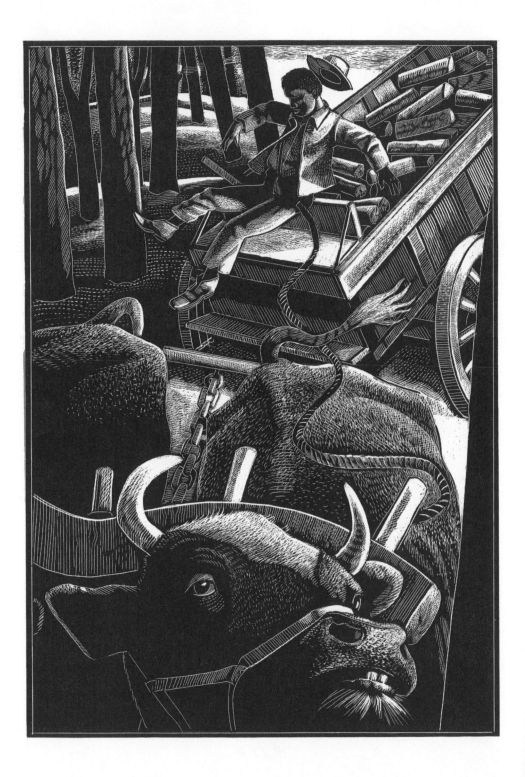

short day, I escaped death by the merest chance.

On my return, I told Mr. Covey what had happened, and how it happened. He ordered me to return to the woods again immediately. I did so, and he followed on after me. Just as I got into the woods, he came up and told me to stop my cart, and that he would teach me how to trifle away my time, and break gates. He then went to a large gum-tree, and with his axe cut three large switches, and, after trimming them up neatly with his pocketknife, he ordered me to take off my clothes. I made him no answer, but stood with my clothes on. He repeated his order. I still made him no answer, nor did I move to strip myself.

Upon this he rushed at me with the fierceness of a tiger, tore off my clothes, and lashed me till he had worn out his switches, cutting me so savagely as to leave the marks visible for a long time. This whipping was the first of a number just like it, and for similar offences.

I lived with Mr. Covey one year. During the first six months of that year, scarce a week passed without his whipping me. I was seldom free from a sore back. We were worked fully up to the point of endurance. Long before day we were up, our horses fed, and by the first approach of day we were off to the field with our hoes and ploughing teams. Mr. Covey gave us enough to eat, but scarce time to eat it. We were often less than five minutes taking our meals. We were often in the field from the first approach of day till its last lingering ray. Midnight often caught us in the field binding blades.*

We were worked in all weathers. It was never too hot or too cold; it could never rain, blow, hail, or snow, too hard for

*Tying the cut grain into bundles.

us to work in the field. Work, work, work, was scarcely more the order of the day than of the night. The longest days were too short for him, and the shortest nights too long for him. I was somewhat unmanageable when I first went there, but a few months of this discipline tamed me.

Mr. Covey succeeded in breaking me. My natural elasticity was crushed, my intellect languished, the disposition to read departed, the cheerful spark that lingered about my eye died; the dark night of slavery closed in upon me, and behold a man transformed into a brute!

FIVE

Sunday is Frederick's only leisure time. He spends the day in a "beast-like stupor" under a large tree overlooking Chesapeake Bay. His spirit is broken. He still serves Edward Covey, who delights in spying on the slaves in the fields, trying to catch them at rest or enjoying themselves. Covey seems to be everywhere at once. He hides behind trees and fence posts. He watches through windows from the house. He crawls on his hands and knees to conceal himself as he tries to find slaves who are shirking their duty. Frederick is exhausted, and he feels completely trapped.

I have often, in the deep stillness of a summer's Sabbath, stood all alone upon the lofty banks of that noble bay, and traced, with saddened heart and tearful eye, the countless number of sails moving off to the mighty ocean. The sight of these always affected me powerfully. My thoughts would compel utterance; and there, with no audience but the Almighty, I would pour out my soul's complaint, in my rude way, with an apostrophe to the moving multitude of ships:

"You are loosed from your moorings, and are free; I am fast in my chains, and am a slave! You move merrily before the gentle gale, and I sadly before the bloody whip! You are freedom's swift-winged angels, that fly round the world; I am confined in bands of iron! O that I were free! O, that I were on one of your gallant decks, and under your protecting wing! Alas! betwixt me and you, the turbid waters roll. Go on, go on. O that I could also go! Could I but swim! If I could fly! O, why was I born a man, of whom to make a brute! The glad ship is gone; she hides in the dim distance. I am left in the hottest hell of unending slavery. O God, save me! God, deliver me! Let me be free! Is there any God? Why am I a slave? I will run away. I will not stand it. Get caught, or get clear, I'll try it. I had as well die with ague as the fever. I have only one life to lose. I had as well be killed running as die standing. Only think of it; one hundred miles straight north, and I am free! Try it? Yes! God helping me, I will. It cannot be that I shall live and die a slave. I will take to the water. This very bay shall yet bear me into freedom."

ON ONE OF THE HOTTEST DAYS of the month of August, 1833, Bill Smith, William Hughes, a slave named Eli, and myself, were engaged in fanning wheat. I was carrying wheat to the fan. The work was simple, requiring strength rather than intellect; yet, to one entirely unused to such work, it came very hard. About three o'clock of that day, I broke down; my strength failed me; I was seized with a violent aching of the head, attended with extreme dizziness; I trembled in every limb. When I could stand no longer, I fell, and felt as if held down by an immense weight.

The fan of course stopped; every one had his own work to do; and no one could do the work of the other, and have his own go on at the same time.

Mr. Covey was at the house, about one hundred yards from the treading-yard where we were fanning. On hearing the fan stop, he left immediately, and came to the spot where we were. He hastily inquired what the matter was. Bill answered that I was sick, and there was no one to bring wheat to the fan. I had by this time crawled away under the side of the post and rail-fence by which the yard was enclosed, hoping to find relief by getting out of the sun. He then asked where I was. He was told by one of the hands. He came to the spot, and, after looking at me awhile, asked me what was the matter. I told him as well as I could, for I scarce had strength to speak. He then gave me a savage kick in the side, and told me to get up. I tried to do so, but fell back in the attempt. He gave me another kick, and again told me to rise. I again tried, and succeeded in gaining my feet; but, stooping to get the tub with which I was feeding the fan, I again staggered and fell. Mr. Covey took up the hickory slat with which Hughes had been striking off the half-bushel measure, and with it gave me a heavy blow upon the head, making a large wound, and the blood ran freely; and with this again told me to get up. I made no effort to comply, having now made up my mind to let him do his worst. In a short time after receiving this blow, my head grew better. Mr. Covey had now left me to my fate.

At this moment I resolved, for the first time, to go to my master, enter a complaint, and ask his protection. In order to do this, I must that afternoon walk seven miles; and this, under the circumstances, was truly a severe undertaking. I was exceedingly feeble; made so as much by the kicks and blows which

I received, as by the severe fit of sickness to which I had been subjected.

I, however, watched my chance, while Covey was looking in an opposite direction, and started for St. Michael's: I succeeded in getting a considerable distance on my way to the woods, when Covey discovered me, and called after me to come back, threatening what he would do if I did not come.

I disregarded both his calls and his threats, and made my way to the woods as fast as my feeble state would allow; and thinking I might be overhauled by him if I kept the road, I walked through the woods, keeping far enough from the road to avoid detection, and near enough to prevent losing my way. I had not gone far before my little strength again failed me. I could go no farther. I fell down, and lay for a considerable time. The blood was yet oozing from the wound on my head. For a time I thought I should bleed to death; and think now that I should have done so, but that the blood so matted my hair as to stop the wound.

After lying there about three quarters of an hour, I nerved myself up again, and started on my way, through bogs and briers, barefooted and bareheaded, tearing my feet sometimes at nearly every step; and after a journey of about seven miles, occupying some five hours to perform it, I arrived at master's store. I then presented an appearance enough to affect any but a heart of iron. From the crown of my head to my feet, I was covered with blood. My hair was all clotted with dust and blood; my shirt was stiff with blood. My legs and feet were torn in sundry places with briers and thorns, and were also covered with blood. I suppose I looked like a man who had escaped a den of wild beasts, and barely escaped them. In this state I appeared before my master, humbly entreating him to interpose his authority for my protection. I told him all the circumstances as well as I could, and it seemed, as I spoke, at times to affect him. He would then walk the floor, and seek to justify Covey by saying he expected I deserved it. He asked me what I wanted. I told him, to let me get a new home; that as sure as I lived with Mr. Covey again, I should live with but to die with him; that Covey would surely kill me; he was in a fair way for it.

Master Thomas ridiculed the idea that there was any danger of Mr. Covey's killing me, and said that he knew Mr. Covey, that he was a good man, and that he could not think of taking me from him; that, should he do so, he would lose the whole year's wages; that I belonged to Mr. Covey for one year, and that I must go back to him, come what might; and that I must not trouble him with any more stories, or that he would himself *get hold of me.*

After threatening me thus, he gave me a very large dose of salts, telling me that I might remain in St. Michael's that night, (it being quite late,) but that I must be off back to Mr. Covey's early in the morning; and that if I did not, he would *get hold of me,* which meant that he would whip me. I remained all night, and, according to his orders, I started off to Covey's in the morning, (Saturday morning,) wearied in body and broken in spirit. I got no supper that night, or breakfast that morning.

I reached Covey's about nine o'clock; and just as I was getting over the fence that divided Mrs. Kemp's fields from ours, out ran Covey with his cowskin, to give me another whipping. Before he could reach me, I succeeded in getting to the corn-field; and as the corn was very high, it afforded me the means of hiding. He seemed very angry, and searched for me a long time. My behavior was altogether unaccountable. He finally gave up the chase, thinking, I suppose, that I must come home for something to eat; he would give himself no further trouble in looking for me. I spent that day mostly in the woods, having the alternative before me—to go home and be whipped to death, or stay in the woods and be starved to death.

That night, I fell in with Sandy Jenkins, a slave with whom I was somewhat acquainted. Sandy had a free wife who lived about four miles from Mr. Covey's; and it being Saturday, he was on his way to see her. I told him my circumstances, and he very kindly invited me to go home with him. I went home with him, and talked this whole matter over, and got his advice as to what course it was best for me to pursue. He told me, with great solemnity, I must go back to Covey; but that before I went, I must go with him into another part of the woods, where there was a certain *root*, which, if I would take some of it with me, carrying it *always on my right side*, would render it impossible for Mr. Covey, or any other white man, to whip me.

I IMMEDIATELY STARTED for home; and upon entering the yard gate, out came Mr. Covey on his way to meeting. He spoke to me very kindly, bade me drive the pigs from a lot near by, and passed on towards the church. Now, this singular conduct of Mr. Covey really made me begin to think that there was something in the *root* which Sandy had given me.

All went well till Monday morning. On this morning, the virtue of the *root* was fully tested. Long before daylight, I was called to go and rub, curry, and feed, the horses. I obeyed, and was glad to obey. But whilst thus engaged, whilst in the act of throwing down some blades from the loft, Mr. Covey entered the stable with a long rope; and just as I was half out of the loft, he caught hold of my legs, and was about tying me. As soon as I found what he was up to, I gave a sudden spring, and as I did so, he holding to my legs, I was brought sprawling on the stable floor. Mr. Covey seemed now to think he had me, and could do what he pleased; but at this moment—from whence came the spirit I don't know—I resolved to fight; and, suiting my action to the resolution, I seized Covey hard by the throat; and as I did so, I rose. He held on to me, and I to him. My resistance was so entirely unexpected, that Covey seemed taken all aback. He trembled like a leaf. This gave me assurance, and I held him uneasy, causing the blood to run where I touched him with the ends of my fingers.

Mr. Covey soon called out to Hughes for help. Hughes came, and, while Covey held me, attempted to tie my right hand. While he was in the act of doing so, I watched my chance, and gave him a heavy kick close under the ribs. This kick fairly sickened Hughes, so that he left me in the hands of Mr. Covey. This kick had the effect of not only weakening Hughes, but Covey also. When he saw Hughes bending over with pain, his courage quailed. He asked me if I meant to persist in my resistance. I told him I did, come what might; that he had used me like a brute for six months, and that I was determined to be used so no longer.

With that, he strove to drag me to a stick that was lying just out of the stable door. He meant to knock me down. But just as he was leaning over to get the stick, I seized him with both hands by his collar, and brought him by a sudden snatch to the ground. By this time, Bill came. Covey called upon him for assistance. Bill wanted to know what he could do. Covey said, "Take hold of him, take hold of him!" Bill said his master hired him out to work, and not to help to whip me; so he left Covey and myself to fight our own battle out.

We were at it for nearly two hours. Covey at length let me

go, puffing and blowing at a great rate, saying that if I had not resisted, he would not have whipped me half so much. The truth was, that he had not whipped me at all. I considered him as getting entirely the worst end of the bargain; for he had drawn no blood from me, but I had from him. The whole six months afterwards, that I spent with Mr. Covey, he never laid the weight of his finger upon me in anger. He would occasionally say, he didn't want to get hold of me again. "No," thought I, "you need not; for you will come off worse than you did before."

From this time I was never again what might be called fairly whipped, though I remained a slave four years afterwards. I had several fights, but was never whipped.

This battle with Mr. Covey was the turning-point in my career as a slave. It rekindled the few expiring embers of freedom, and revived within me a sense of my own manhood. It recalled the departed self-confidence, and inspired me again with a determination to be free.

$\mathcal{SIX}$

FREDERICK'S TIME with Covey will soon come to an end. After the holidays he will be hired out to work at a nearby farm operated by William Freeland, and on an adjacent farm owned by a man Frederick calls Mr. William Hamilton (actually named Hambleton).

Frederick will find better conditions at these farms. He will begin to take pride in his growing physical strength and manhood while he makes strong friendships with slaves his age. He will also discover the joy of teaching other slaves to read. But he is increasingly determined to be free.

My term of actual service to Mr. Edward Covey ended on Christmas day, 1833. The days between Christmas and New Year's day are allowed as holidays; and, accordingly, we were not required to perform any labor. This time we regarded as our own, by the grace of our masters; and we therefore used or abused it nearly as we pleased. The staid, sober, thinking and industrious ones of our number would employ themselves in making corn-brooms, mats, horse-collars, and baskets; and another class of us would spend the time in hunting opossums, hares, and coons.

But by far the larger part engaged in such sports and merriments as playing ball, wrestling, running foot-races, fiddling, dancing, and drinking whiskey; and this latter mode of spending the time was by far the most agreeable to the feelings of our masters. A slave who would work during the holidays was considered by our masters as scarcely deserving them. He was regarded as one who rejected the favor of his master. It was deemed a disgrace not to get drunk at Christmas; and he was regarded as lazy indeed, who had not provided himself with the necessary means, during the year, to get whiskey enough to last him through Christmas.

From what I know of the effect of these holidays upon the slave, I believe them to be among the most effective means in the hands of the slaveholder in keeping down the spirit of insurrection. Were the slaveholders at once to abandon this practice, I have not the slightest doubt it would lead to an immediate insurrection among the slaves. These holidays serve as conductors, or safety-valves, to carry off the rebellious spirit of enslaved humanity. But for these, the slave would be forced up to the wildest desperation; and woe betide the slaveholder, the day he ventures to remove or hinder the operation of these conductors! I warn him that, in such an event, a spirit will go forth in their midst, more to be dreaded than the most appalling earthquake.

ON THE FIRST OF JANUARY, 1834, I left Mr. Covey, and went to live with Mr. William Freeland, who lived about three miles from St. Michael's. I soon found Mr. Freeland a very different man from Mr. Covey. Though not rich, he was what would be called an educated southern gentleman. He, like Mr. Covey, gave us enough to eat; but, unlike Mr. Covey, he also gave us sufficient time to take our meals. He worked us hard, but always between sunrise and sunset. My treatment, while in his employment, was heavenly, compared with what I experienced at the hands of Mr. Edward Covey.

Mr. Freeland was himself the owner of but two slaves. Their names were Henry Harris and John Harris. The rest of his hands he hired. These consisted of myself, Sandy Jenkins, and Handy Caldwell. Henry and John were quite intelligent, and in a very little while after I went there, I succeeded in creating in them a strong desire to learn how to read. This desire soon sprang up in the others also. They very soon mustered up some old spelling-books, and nothing would do but that I must keep a Sabbath school. I agreed to do so, and accordingly devoted my Sundays to teaching these my loved fellow-slaves how to read.

I held my Sabbath school at the house of a free colored man. I had at one time over forty scholars, and those of the right sort, ardently desiring to learn. The work of instructing my dear fellow-slaves was the sweetest engagement with which I was ever blessed.

The year passed off smoothly. At the close of the year 1834, Mr. Freeland again hired me of my master, for the year 1835. But, by this time, I began to want to live *upon free land* as well as *with Freeland;* and I was no longer content, therefore, to live with him or any other slaveholder. I began, with the com-

mencement of the year, to prepare myself for a final struggle, which should decide my fate one way or the other. I was fast approaching manhood, and year after year had passed, and I was still a slave. These thoughts roused me—I must do something. But I was not willing to cherish this determination alone. My fellow-slaves were dear to me. I was anxious to have them participate with me in this, my life-giving determination. I bent myself to devising ways and means for our escape, and meanwhile strove, on all fitting occasions, to impress them with the gross fraud and inhumanity of slavery. I never loved any or confided in any people more than my fellow-slaves, and especially those with whom I lived at Mr. Freeland's. I believe we would have died for each other.

The plan we finally concluded upon was, to get a large canoe belonging to Mr. Hamilton, and upon the Saturday night previous to Easter holidays, paddle directly up the Chesapeake Bay. On our arrival at the head of the bay, a distance of seventy or eighty miles from where we lived, it was our purpose to turn our canoe adrift, and follow the guidance of the north star till we got to the limits of Maryland. Our reason for taking the water route was, that we were less liable to be suspected as runaways; we hoped to be regarded as fishermen; whereas, if we should take the land route, we should be subjected to interruptions of almost every kind. Any one having a white face, and being so disposed, could stop us, and subject us to examination.

The week before our intended start, I wrote several protections, one for each of us. As well as I can remember, they were in the following words, to wit:

"This is to certify that I, the undersigned, have given the bearer, my servant, full liberty to go to Baltimore, and spend the Easter holidays. Written with mine own hand, &c., 1835.
"WILLIAM HAMILTON,
"Near St. Michael's, in Talbot county, Maryland."

Friday night was a sleepless one for me. I probably felt more anxious than the rest, because I was, by common consent, at the head of the whole affair. The first two hours of that morning were such as I never experienced before, and hope never to again. We were spreading manure; and all at once, while thus engaged, I was overwhelmed with an indescribable feeling, in the fulness of which I turned to Sandy, who was near by, and said, "We are betrayed!" "Well," said he, "that thought has this moment struck me." We said no more. I was never more certain of any thing.

The horn was blown as usual, and we went up from the field to the house for breakfast. Just as I got to the house, in looking out at the lane gate, I saw four white men, with two colored men. The white men were on horseback, and the colored ones were walking behind, as if tied. I watched them a few moments till they got up to our lane gate. Here they halted, and tied the colored men to the gate-post. I was not yet certain as to what the matter was. In a few moments, in rode Mr. Hamilton, with a speed betokening great excitement. He came to the door, and inquired if Master William was in. He was told he was at the barn. Mr. Hamilton, without dismounting, rode up to the barn with extraordinary speed. In a few moments, he and Mr. Freeland returned to the house. By this time, the three constables rode up, and in great haste dismounted, tied their horses, and met Master William and Mr. Hamilton returning from the barn; and after talking awhile, they all walked up to the kitchen door. There was no one in the kitchen but myself and John. Henry and Sandy were up at the barn.

Mr. Freeland put his head in at the door, and called me by name, saying, there were some gentlemen at the door who wished to see me. I stepped to the door, and inquired what they wanted. They at once seized me, and, without giving me any satisfaction, tied me—lashing my hands closely together. I insisted upon knowing what the matter was. They at length said, that they had learned I had been in a "scrape," and that I was to be examined before my master; and if their information proved false, I should not be hurt.

In a few moments, they succeeded in tying John. Then they turned to Henry, who had by this time returned, and commanded him to cross his hands. "I won't!" said Henry, in a firm tone, indicating his readiness to meet the consequences of his refusal. "Won't you?" said Tom Graham, the constable. "No, I won't!" said Henry, in a still stronger tone. With this, two of the constables pulled out their shining pistols, and swore, by their Creator, that they would make him cross his hands or kill him. Each cocked his pistol, and, with fingers on the trigger, walked up to Henry, saying, at the same time, if he did not cross his hands, they would blow his damned heart out. "Shoot me, shoot me!" said Henry; "you can't kill me but once. Shoot, shoot—and be damned! *I won't be tied!*" This he said in a tone of loud defiance. At the same time, with a motion as quick as lightning, he with one single stroke dashed the pistols from the hand of each constable. As he did this, all hands fell upon him, and, after beating him some time, they finally overpowered him, and got him tied. During the scuffle, I managed, I know not how, to get my pass out, and, without being discovered, put it into the fire.

We were all now tied; and just as we were to leave for Easton jail, Betsy Freeland, mother of William Freeland, came to the door with her hands full of biscuits, and divided them between Henry and John. She then delivered herself of a speech, to the following effect—addressing herself to me, she said, "*You devil! You yellow devil!* it was you that put it into the heads of Henry and John to run away. But for you, you long-legged mulatto devil! Henry nor John would never have thought of such a thing." I made no reply, and was immediately hurried off towards St. Michael's. Just a moment previous to the scuffle with Henry, Mr. Hamilton suggested the propriety of making a search for the protections which he had understood Frederick had written for himself and the rest. But, just at the moment he was about carrying his proposal into effect, his aid was needed in helping to tie Henry; and the excitement attending the scuffle caused them either to forget, or to deem it unsafe, under the circumstances, to search. So we were not yet convicted of the intention to run away.

We were to be dragged that morning fifteen miles behind horses, and then to be placed in the Easton jail. When we reached St. Michael's, we underwent a sort of examination. We all denied that we ever intended to run away. We did this more to bring out the evidence against us, than from any hope of getting clear of being sold; for, as I have said, we were ready for that. The fact was, we cared but little where we went, so we went together. Our greatest concern was about separation. We dreaded that more than any thing this side of death. We found the evidence against us to be the testimony of one person; our master would not tell who it was; but we came to a unanimous decision among ourselves as to who their informant was. We were delivered up to the sheriff, Mr. Joseph Graham, and by him placed in jail. Henry, John, and myself, were placed in one room together—Charles, and Henry Bailey, in another. Their object in separating us was to hinder concert.

We had been in jail scarcely twenty minutes, when a swarm of slave traders, and agents for slave traders, flocked into jail to look at us, and to ascertain if we were for sale. Such a set of beings I never saw before! I felt myself surrounded by so many fiends from perdition. A band of pirates never looked more like their father, the devil. They laughed and grinned over us, saying, "Ah, my boys! we have got you, haven't we?" And after taunting us in various ways, they one by one went into an examination of us, with intent to ascertain our value. They would impudently ask us if we would not like to have them for our masters. We would make them no answer, and leave them to find out as best they could. Then they would curse and swear at us, telling us that they could take the devil out of us in a very little while, if we were only in their hands.

Immediately after the holidays, Mr. Hamilton and Mr. Freeland came up to Easton, and took Charles, the two Henrys, and John, out of jail, leaving me alone. I regarded this separation as a final one. It caused me more pain than any thing else in the whole transaction. I was ready for any thing rather than separation.

SEVEN

FREDERICK IS NOW SEEN as a troublemaker and a dangerous influence on the other farm slaves. Thomas Auld fears for his young slave's life after the attempted escape, for Mr. Hambleton says that he will shoot Frederick on sight if he is not taken away. So Frederick will be permitted to return to live with Hugh Auld in Baltimore, a city which is home to about one-fourth of Maryland's free blacks. Here most former slaves work in the trades, and many who are still slaves are allowed to hire themselves out for pay. Frederick is eager for the opportunity to learn a trade as he secretly prepares for a life of freedom.

I was now left to my fate. I was all alone, and within the walls of a stone prison. But a few days before, and I was full of hope. I expected to have been safe in a land of freedom; but now I was covered with gloom, sunk down to the utmost despair. I thought the possibility of freedom was gone. I was kept in this way for about one week, at the end of which, Captain Auld, my master, to my surprise and utter astonishment, came up, and took me out, with the intention of sending me, with a gentleman of his acquaintance, into Alabama. But, for some cause or other, he did not send me to Alabama, but concluded to send me back to Baltimore, to live again with his brother Hugh, and to learn a trade.

In a few weeks after I went to Baltimore, Master Hugh hired me to Mr. William Gardner, an extensive ship-builder, on Fell's Point. I was put there to learn how to calk. It, however, proved a very unfavorable place for the accomplishment of this object. In entering the shipyard, my orders from Mr. Gardner were, to do whatever the carpenters commanded me to do.

At times I needed a dozen pair of hands. I was called a dozen ways in the space of a single minute. Three or four voices would strike my ear at the same moment. It was—"Fred., come help me to cant this timber here."—"Fred., come carry this timber yonder."—"Fred., bring that roller here."—"Fred., go get a fresh can of water."—"Fred., come help me saw off the end of this timber."—"Fred., go quick, and get the crowbar."—"Fred., hold on the end of this fall."—"Fred., go to the blacksmith's shop, and get a new punch."—"Hurra, Fred.! Run and bring me a cold chisel."—"I say, Fred., bear a hand, and get up a fire as quick as lightning under that steambox."—"Halloo, nigger! come turn this grindstone."—"Come, come! move, move! and *bowse* this timber forward."—"I say, darky, blast your eyes, why don't you heat up some pitch?"—"Halloo! halloo! halloo!" (Three voices at the same time.) "Come here!—Go there!—Hold on where you are! Damn you, if you move, I'll knock your brains out!"

This was my school for eight months; and I might have remained there longer, but for a most horrid fight I had with four or five white apprentices, in which my left eye was nearly knocked out, and I was horribly mangled in other respects. The facts in the case were these: Until a very little while after I went there, white and black ship-carpenters worked side by side, and no one seemed to see any impropriety in it. All hands seemed to be very well satisfied. Many of the black carpenters were freemen. Things seemed to be going on very well. All at once, the white carpenters knocked off, and said they would not work with free colored workmen. Their reason for this, as alleged, was, that if the free colored carpenters were encouraged, they would soon take the trade into their own hands, and poor white men would be thrown out of employment.

They therefore felt called upon at once to put a stop to it. And, taking advantage of Mr. Gardner's necessities, they broke off, swearing they would work no longer, unless he would discharge his black carpenters. Now, though this did not extend to me in form, it did reach me in fact. My fellow-apprentices very soon began to feel it degrading to them to work with me. They began to put on airs, and talk about the "niggers" taking the country, saying we all ought to be killed; and, being encouraged by the journeymen, they commenced making my condition as hard as they could, by hectoring me around, and sometimes striking me. I, of course, kept the vow I made after the fight with Mr. Covey, and struck back again, regardless of consequences. While I kept them from combining, I succeeded very well; for I could whip the whole of them, taking them separately. They, however, at length combined, and came upon me, armed with sticks, stones, and heavy handspikes.

One came in front of me with a half brick. There was one at each side of me, and one behind me. While I was attending

to those in front, and on either side, the one behind ran up with the handspike, and struck me a heavy blow upon the head. It stunned me. I fell, and with this they all ran upon me, and fell to beating me with their fists. I let them lay on for a while, gathering strength. In an instant, I gave a sudden surge, and rose to my hands and knees. Just as I did that, one of their number gave me, with his heavy boot, a powerful kick in the left eye. My eyeball seemed to have burst. When they saw my eye closed, and badly swollen, they left me. With this I seized the handspike, and for a time pursued them. But here the carpenters interfered, and I thought I might as well give it up. It was impossible to stand my hand against so many. All this took place in sight of not less than fifty white ship-carpenters, and not one interposed a friendly word; but some cried, "Kill the damned nigger! Kill him! kill him! He struck a white person." I found my only chance for life was in flight. I succeeded in getting away without an additional blow, and barely so; for to strike a white man is death by Lynch law—and that was the law in Mr. Gardner's ship-yard; nor is there much of any other out of Mr. Gardner's ship-yard.

I went directly home, and told the story of my wrongs to Master Hugh; and I am happy to say of him, irreligious as he was, his conduct was heavenly, compared with that of his brother Thomas under similar circumstances. He listened attentively to my narration of the circumstances leading to the savage outrage, and gave many proofs of his strong indignation at it. The heart of my once overkind mistress was again melted into pity. My puffed-out eye and blood-covered face moved her to tears. She took a chair by me, washed the blood from my face, and, with a mother's tenderness, bound up my head, covering the wounded eye with a lean piece of fresh beef. It was almost compensation for my suffering to witness, once more, a manifestation of kindness from this, my once affectionate old mistress.

Master Hugh, finding he could get no redress, refused to let me go back again to Mr. Gardner. He kept me himself, and his wife dressed my wound till I was again restored to health. He then took me into the ship-yard of which he was foreman. There I was immediately set to calking, and very soon learned the art of using my mallet and irons. In the course of one year from the time I left Mr. Gardner's, I was able to command the highest wages given to the most experienced calkers. I was now of some importance to my master. I was bringing him from six to seven dollars per week.

After learning how to calk, I sought my own employment, made my own contracts, and collected the money which I earned. My pathway became much more smooth than before; my condition was now much more comfortable. When I could get no calking to do, I did nothing. During these leisure times, those old notions about freedom would steal over me again.

In the early part of the year 1838, I became quite restless. I could see no reason why I should, at the end of each week, pour the reward of my toil into the purse of my master. When I carried to him my weekly wages, he would, after counting the money, look me in the face with a robber-like fierceness, and ask, "Is this all?"

EIGHT

FREDERICK HAS MET Anna Murray, a free black woman who works in domestic service, and he intends to marry her. But as a slave he will never be allowed to live with her. Desperate to escape, he plots with Anna for her to follow him north. His next attempt at freedom will succeed. However, Frederick avoids sharing any details of the escape, for the reasons he gives below. The full story of his escape is told in the Epilogue at the end of this book.

I now come to that part of my life during which I planned, and finally succeeded in making, my escape from slavery. But before narrating any of the peculiar circumstances, I deem it proper to make known my intention not to state all the facts connected with the transaction. My reasons for pursuing this course may be understood from the following: First, were I to give a minute statement of all the facts, it is not only possible, but quite probable, that others would thereby be involved in the most embarrassing difficulties. Secondly, such a statement would most undoubtedly induce greater vigilance on the part of slaveholders than has existed heretofore among them; which would, of course, be the means of guarding a door whereby some dear brother bondman might escape his galling chains.

EARLY ON MONDAY MORNING, before Master Hugh had time to make any engagement for me, I went out and got employ-ment of Mr. Butler, at his ship-yard near the drawbridge, upon what is called the City Block, thus making it unnecessary for him to seek employment for me. At the end of the week, I brought him between eight and nine dollars. He seemed very well pleased, and asked why I did not do the same the week before. He little knew what my plans were. My object in work-ing steadily was to remove any suspicion he might entertain of my intent to run away; and in this I succeeded admirably.

Things went on without very smoothly indeed, but within there was trouble. It is impossible for me to describe my feelings as the time of my contemplated start drew near. I had a number of warm-hearted friends in Baltimore—friends that I loved al-most as I did my life—and the thought of being separated from them forever was painful beyond expression.

I felt assured that, if I failed in this attempt, my case would be a hopeless one—it would seal my life as a slave forever. I could not hope to get off with any thing less than the severest punishment, and being placed beyond the means of escape. I remained firm, and, according to my resolution, on the third day of September, 1838, I left my chains, and succeeded in reaching New York without the slightest interruption of any kind. How I did so—what means I adopted—what direction I travelled, and by what mode of conveyance—I must leave unexplained, for the reasons before mentioned.

I HAVE BEEN FREQUENTLY ASKED how I felt when I found myself in a free State. I have never been able to answer the question with any satisfaction to myself. It was a moment of the highest excitement I ever experienced.

In writing to a dear friend, immediately after my arrival at New York, I said I felt like one who had escaped a den of hungry lions. This state of mind, however, very soon subsided; and I was again seized with a feeling of great insecurity and loneliness. I was yet liable to be taken back, and subjected to all the tortures of slavery. This in itself was enough to damp the ardor of my enthusiasm. But the loneliness overcame me. There I was in the midst of thousands, and yet a perfect stranger; without home and without friends, in the midst of thousands of my own brethren—children of a common Father, and yet I dared not to unfold to any of them my sad condition. I was afraid to speak to any one for fear of speaking to the wrong one, and thereby falling into the hands of money-loving kidnappers, whose business it was to lie in wait for the panting fugitive, as the ferocious beasts of the forest lie in wait for their prey.

The motto which I adopted when I started from slavery was this—"Trust no man!" I saw in every white man an enemy, and in almost every colored man cause for distrust. It was a most painful situation; to understand it, one must needs experience it, or imagine himself in similar circumstances. Let him be a fugitive slave in a strange land—a land given up to be the hunting-ground for slaveholders—whose inhabitants are legalized kidnappers—where he is every moment subjected to the

terrible liability of being seized upon by his fellowmen, as the hideous crocodile seizes upon his prey!

I say, let him place himself in my situation—without home or friends—without money or credit—wanting shelter, and no one to give it—wanting bread, and no money to buy it—and at the same time let him feel that he is pursued by merciless men-hunters, and in total darkness as to what to do, where to go, or where to stay—perfectly helpless both as to the means of defence and means of escape—in the midst of plenty, yet suffering the terrible gnawings of hunger—in the midst of houses, yet having no home—among fellow-men, yet feeling as if in the midst of wild beasts, whose greediness to swallow up the trembling and half-famished fugitive is only equalled by that with which the monsters of the deep swallow up the helpless fish upon which they subsist.

Thank Heaven, I remained but a short time in this distressed situation. I was relieved from it by the humane hand of Mr. DAVID RUGGLES, whose vigilance, kindness, and perseverance, I shall never forget. I had been in New York but a few days, when Mr. Ruggles sought me out, and very kindly took me to his boarding-house at the corner of Church and Lespenard Streets. Mr. Ruggles was then very deeply engaged in the memorable *Darg* case, as well as attending to a number of other fugitive slaves, devising ways and means for their successful escape; and, though watched and hemmed in on almost every side, he seemed to be more than a match for his enemies.

Very soon after I went to Mr. Ruggles, he wished to know of me where I wanted to go; as he deemed it unsafe for me to remain in New York. I told him I was a calker, and should like to go where I could get work. I thought of going to Canada;

but he decided against it, and in favor of my going to New Bedford, thinking I should be able to get work there at my trade. At this time, Anna, my intended wife, came on; for I wrote to her immediately after my arrival at New York, (notwithstanding my homeless, houseless, and helpless condition,) informing her of my successful flight, and wishing her to come on forthwith.

In a few days after her arrival, Mr. Ruggles called in the Rev. J. W. C. Pennington, who in the presence of Mr. Ruggles, Mrs. Michaels, and two or three others, performed the marriage ceremony, and gave us a certificate.

Upon receiving this certificate, and a five-dollar bill from Mr. Ruggles, I shouldered one part of our baggage, and Anna took up the other, and we set out forthwith to take passage on board of the steamboat John W. Richmond for Newport, on our way to New Bedford.

NINE

FREDERICK AND ANNA reach New Bedford, Massachusetts, and are directed to the house of Mary and Nathan Johnson, by whom they are kindly received. The Johnsons are relatively prosperous and well-respected African Americans who work hard at building relations between the black and white communities. New Bedford is perhaps the best American city at this time for black people, since it has a strong community of independent blacks who are actively working in a variety of trades.

We now began to feel a degree of safety, and to prepare ourselves for the duties and responsibilities of a life of freedom. On the morning after our arrival at New Bedford, while at the breakfast-table, the question arose as to what name I should be called by. The name given me by my mother was, "Frederick Augustus Washington Bailey." I, however, had dispensed with the two middle names long before I left Maryland so that I was generally known by the name of "Frederick

Bailey." I started from Baltimore bearing the name of "Stanley." When I got to New York, I again changed my name to "Frederick Johnson," and thought that would be the last change. But when I got to New Bedford, I found it necessary again to change my name. The reason of this necessity was, that there were so many Johnsons in New Bedford, it was already quite difficult to distinguish between them. I gave Mr. Johnson the privilege of choosing me a name, but told him he must not take from me the name of "Frederick." I must hold on to that, to preserve a sense of my identity. Mr. Johnson had just been reading the "Lady of the Lake," and at once suggested that my name be "Douglass." From that time until now I have been called "Frederick Douglass;" and as I am more widely known by that name than by either of the others, I shall continue to use it as my own.

IN THE AFTERNOON OF THE DAY when I reached New Bedford, I visited the wharves, to take a view of the shipping. Lying at the wharves, and riding in the stream, I saw many ships of the finest model, in the best order, and of the largest size. Added to this, almost every body seemed to be at work, but noiselessly so, compared with what I had been accustomed to in Baltimore. There were no loud songs heard from those engaged in loading and unloading ships. I heard no deep oaths or horrid curses on the laborer. I saw no whipping of men; but all seemed to go smoothly on. Every man appeared to understand his work, and went at it with a sober, yet cheerful earnestness, which betokened the deep interest which he felt in what he was doing, as well as a sense of his own dignity as a man. To me this looked exceedingly strange.

In about four months after I went to New Bedford, there

came a young man to me, and inquired if I did not wish to take the "Liberator." I told him I did; but, just having made my escape from slavery, I remarked that I was unable to pay for it then. I, however, finally became a subscriber to it. The paper came, and I read it from week to week with such feelings as it would be quite idle for me to attempt to describe. The paper became my meat and my drink. My soul was set all on fire. Its sympathy for my brethren in bonds—its scathing denunciations of slaveholders—its faithful exposures of slavery—and its powerful attacks upon the upholders of the institution—sent a thrill of joy through my soul, such as I had never felt before!

While attending an anti-slavery convention at Nantucket, on the 11th of August, 1841,* I felt strongly moved to speak, and was at the same time much urged to do so by Mr. William C. Coffin, a gentleman who had heard me speak in the colored people's meeting at New Bedford. It was a severe cross, and I took it up reluctantly. The truth was, I felt myself a slave, and the idea of speaking to white people weighed me down. I spoke but a few moments, when I felt a degree of freedom, and said what I desired with considerable ease.

From that time until now, I have been engaged in pleading the cause of my brethren—with what success, and with what devotion, I leave those acquainted with my labors to decide.

*August 16, 1841 is the correct date.

Epilogue

To PROTECT OTHER SLAVES, Frederick Douglass avoided telling the readers of his *Narrative* exactly how he had escaped from Baltimore. Before his escape he had assisted many runaways, and he was well aware of the Underground Railroad. This was a network of sympathetic blacks and whites who helped escaping slaves move safely from one household to another on their way north. Frederick could not bring himself to ask directions to these homes because of his fear of slavehunters who could turn him in for a bounty. He was truly on his own.

The full story of Frederick's daring escape is told here.

Through the sale of a feather bed, Anna Murray obtained the money to pay for Frederick's journey north. She altered his clothes carefully so he could pass as a sailor. Frederick wore a red shirt, a kerchief around his neck, and a flat-topped broad-brimmed hat.

Frederick had befriended a free black sailor and through him was able to obtain seaman's papers that would imply that he was not a slave. Because these documents described a man wholly unlike Frederick, it was important that they not be examined carefully by ticket agents. Isaac Rolls, a black friend, drove his horse-drawn cab quickly past the ticket window of the railroad station so Frederick could hop aboard the train just as it was pulling out.

Frederick sat in the crowded "colored car," the only part of the train where blacks were allowed to sit. When the conductor reached him and demanded his free papers, documents that all free blacks had to carry, Frederick answered boldly, "No, sir. I never carry my free papers to sea with me." Instead, he pulled out his seaman's papers and unfolded the documents in a slow and confident manner. The conductor, glancing at the picture of an eagle at the top, returned the papers to Frederick without reading them.

But the danger was not yet past. Frederick had to board a ferry at Havre de Grace to cross the Susquehanna River. There he encountered Henry, the slave of William Freeland, who expressed his amazement at seeing his old friend dressed as a seaman. And Master William himself was sitting nearby! Frederick spun around and prevented Mr. Freeland from recognizing him during the rest of the tense crossing.

Another danger soon presented itself. When Frederick boarded a second northbound train, he sat down and looked casually out the window—into the windows of a southbound train. There, staring blankly in his direction, was a ship's captain who frequented the Baltimore shipyard where Frederick had worked. But Frederick's extraordinary luck held, and the man did not recognize him. The next close call was a searching look from a German blacksmith who knew Frederick but chose not to betray him.

The second train, and another ferry, brought Frederick through the slave state of Delaware to the free cities of Philadelphia and New York. After the terror of his first days in New York, and his enormous relief at making contact with the Underground Railroad, he was reunited with Anna. She had traveled north alone to join him in New York, and together they began their life of freedom in New Bedford, Massachusetts.

Bibliography

ALLEN, THOMAS B. *The Blue and the Gray.* Washington, D.C.: The National Geographic Society, 1992.

DOUGLASS, FREDERICK. *The Narrative of the Life of Frederick Douglass, An American Slave, Written by Himself.* Boston: The Anti-Slavery Office, 1845.

GRAHAM, S. *There Was Once a Slave.* New York: Messner, 1947.

MCFEELEY, WILLIAM S. *Frederick Douglass.* New York: Simon & Schuster, 1991.

FREDERICK DOUGLASS rose from slavery to become the best-known African American of his day, and one of the great figures in American history. Born to a slave mother who died when he was a young child, Douglass learned to read at an early age. He escaped from slavery at the age of twenty and spent the rest of his life working for the cause of freedom. He wrote three autobiographies, including *The Narrative of the Life of Frederick Douglass, an American Slave, Written by Himself*. He died in 1895.

MICHAEL MCCURDY has illustrated many books, including the highly praised *American Tall Tales*, by Mary Pope Osborne, *Giants in the Land*, by Diana Appelbaum, and Howard Norman's *The Owl-Scatterer*, a *New York Times* Best Illustrated Book. He lives with his wife, Deborah, and their two children on an old farm in the Berkshire Hills of Massachusetts.